Ghost
in
a
Four-
Room
Apartment

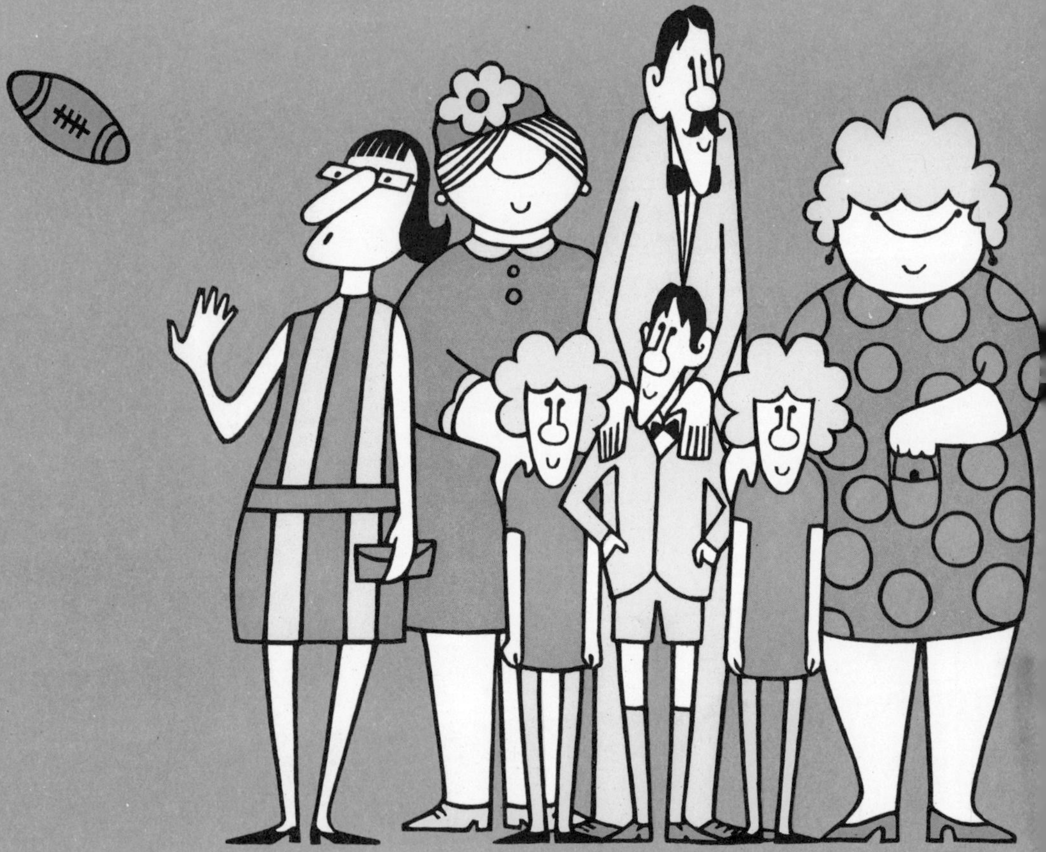

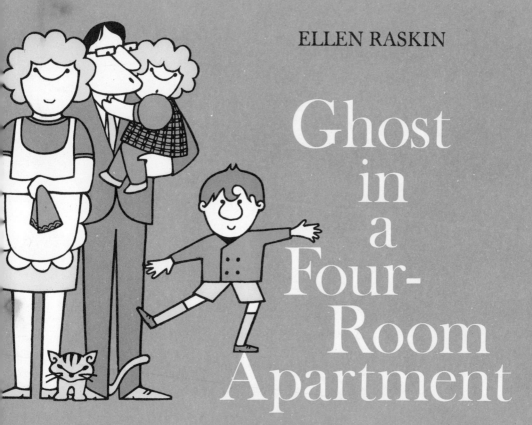

ELLEN RASKIN

Ghost in a Four- Room Apartment

AN ALADDIN BOOK
Atheneum

PUBLISHED BY ATHENEUM
ALL RIGHTS RESERVED
COPYRIGHT © 1969 BY ELLEN RASKIN
PUBLISHED SIMULTANEOUSLY IN CANADA BY
MCCLELLAND & STEWART, LTD.
MANUFACTURED IN THE UNITED STATES OF AMERICA BY
CONNECTICUT PRINTERS, INC., BLOOMFIELD, CONNECTICUT
ISBN 0-689-70446-1
FIRST ALADDIN EDITION

This book is dedicated
to all parents, librarians and teachers
who will read this story aloud
in two voices.

This book is dedicated

to all parents, librarians and teachers

who will read this story aloud

in two voices.

Knock, knock, rap, tap, ring, ring!

You can't see me, but I am here.

You can't see me, you see, because I am a ghost.

In fact, I am a very special ghost.

I am the kind of ghost who raps and taps

and makes the telephone ring when no one's there.

I am a poltergeist!

Ring, ring.

I have come a long way.

Ring, ring.

I have come to visit my friend Horace Homecoming.

Ring, ring, rap, tap, knock, knock...

Here is Horace, good and bad,
Who lives in a four-room apartment.

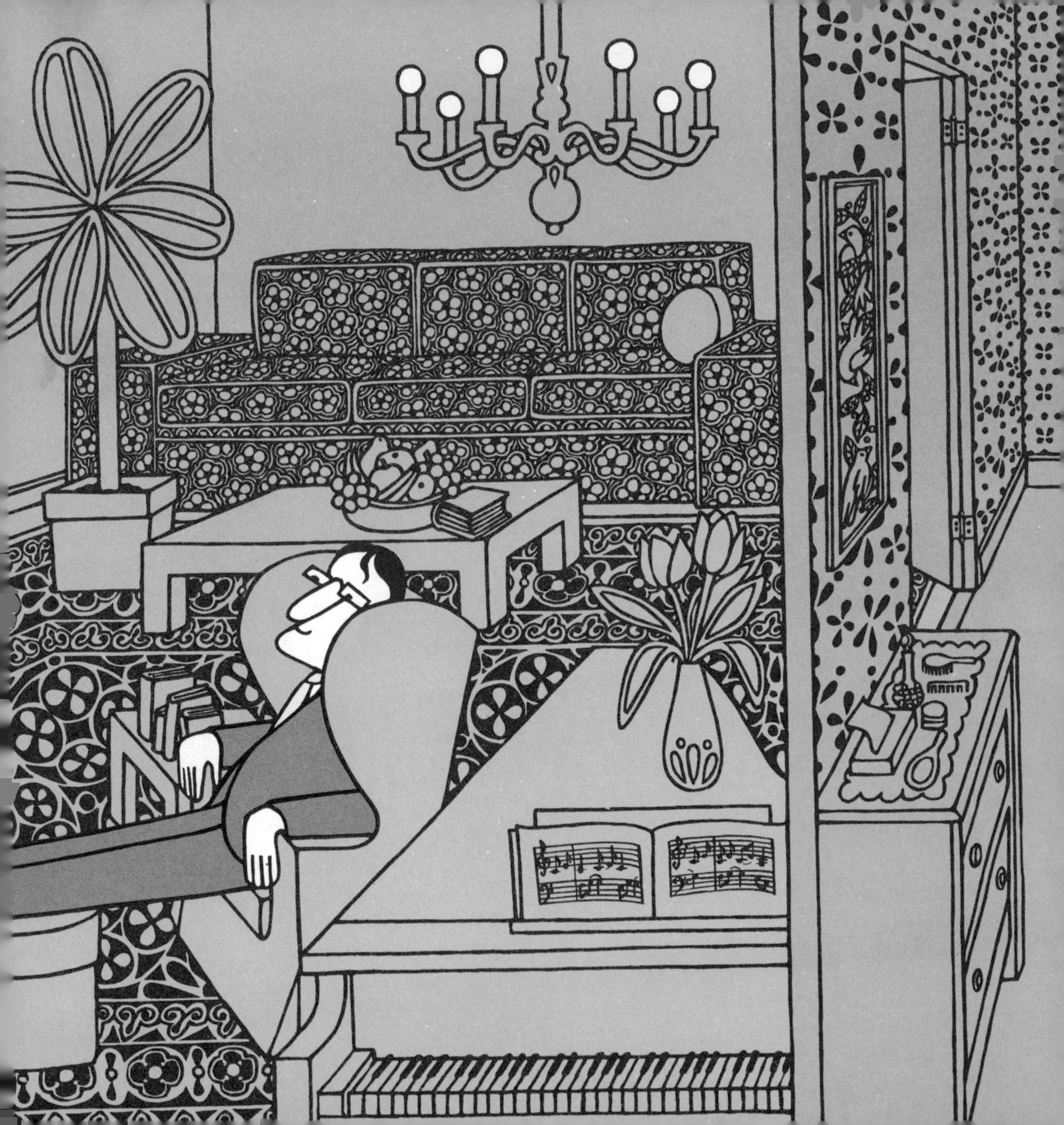

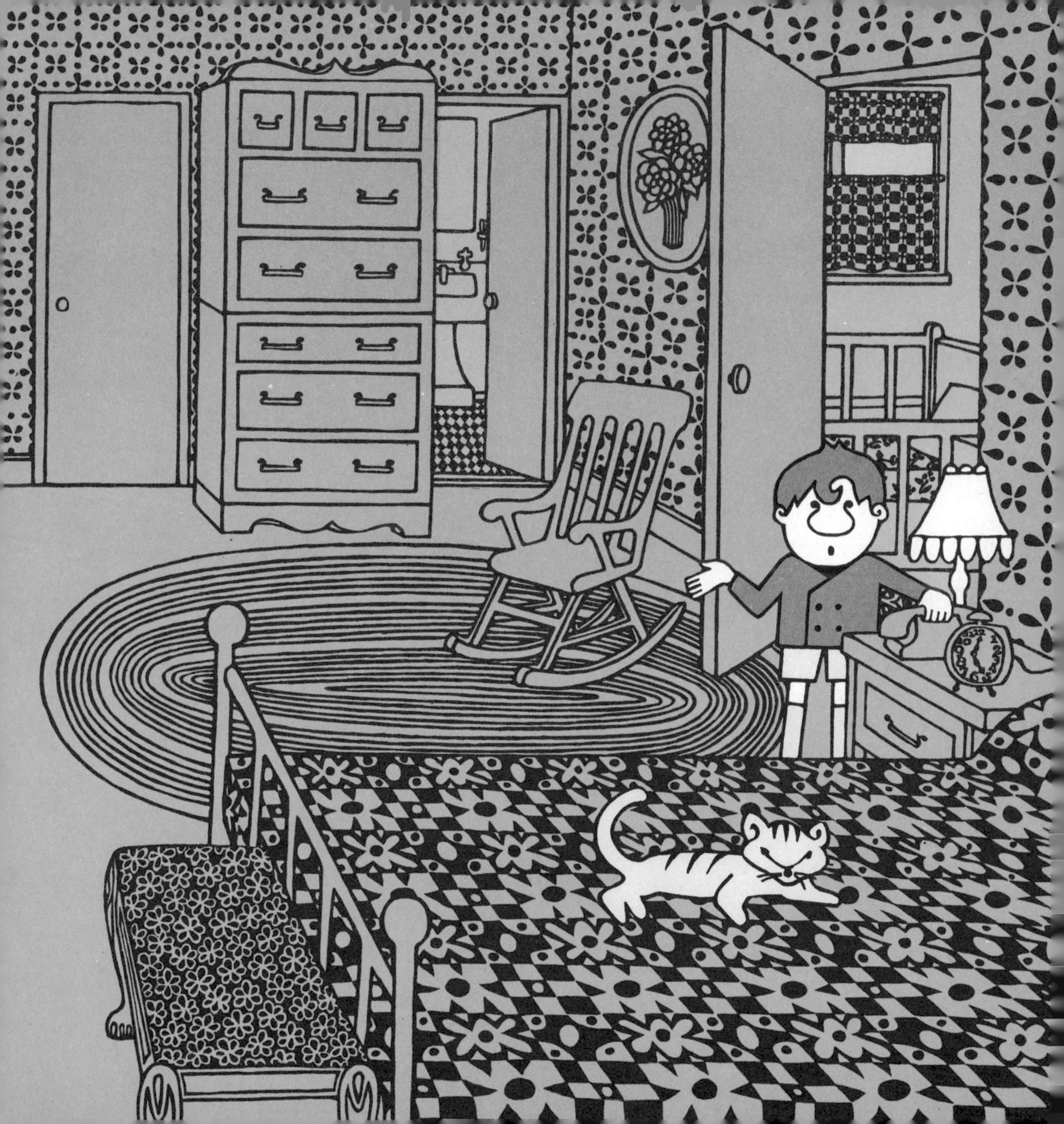

...knock, knock, rap, tap, ring, ring.

Some people don't like poltergeists.

Some people say poltergeists are nuisances

because we make too much noise.

Some people say poltergeists are nuisances

because we throw things like toys and furniture.

Well, we poltergeists don't like some people

who don't like us poltergeists.

We are really fun-loving spirits who only want to play.

We just have our own way of playing.

Watch out Doris! Here I come!

Ring, ring, rap, tap, knock, knock...

Here is Doris, dressed in plaid,
Sister of Horace, good and bad,
Who lives in a four-room apartment.

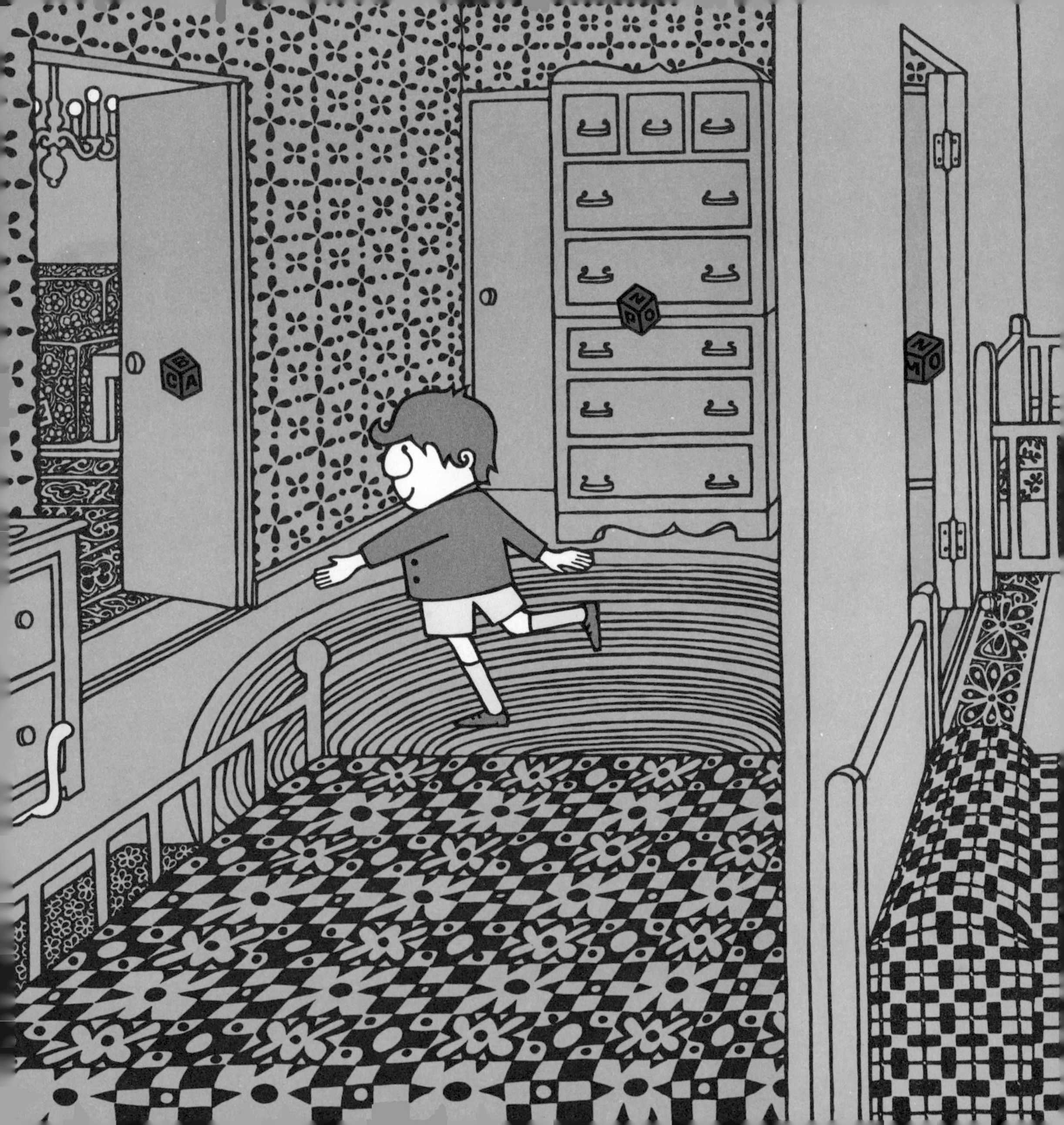

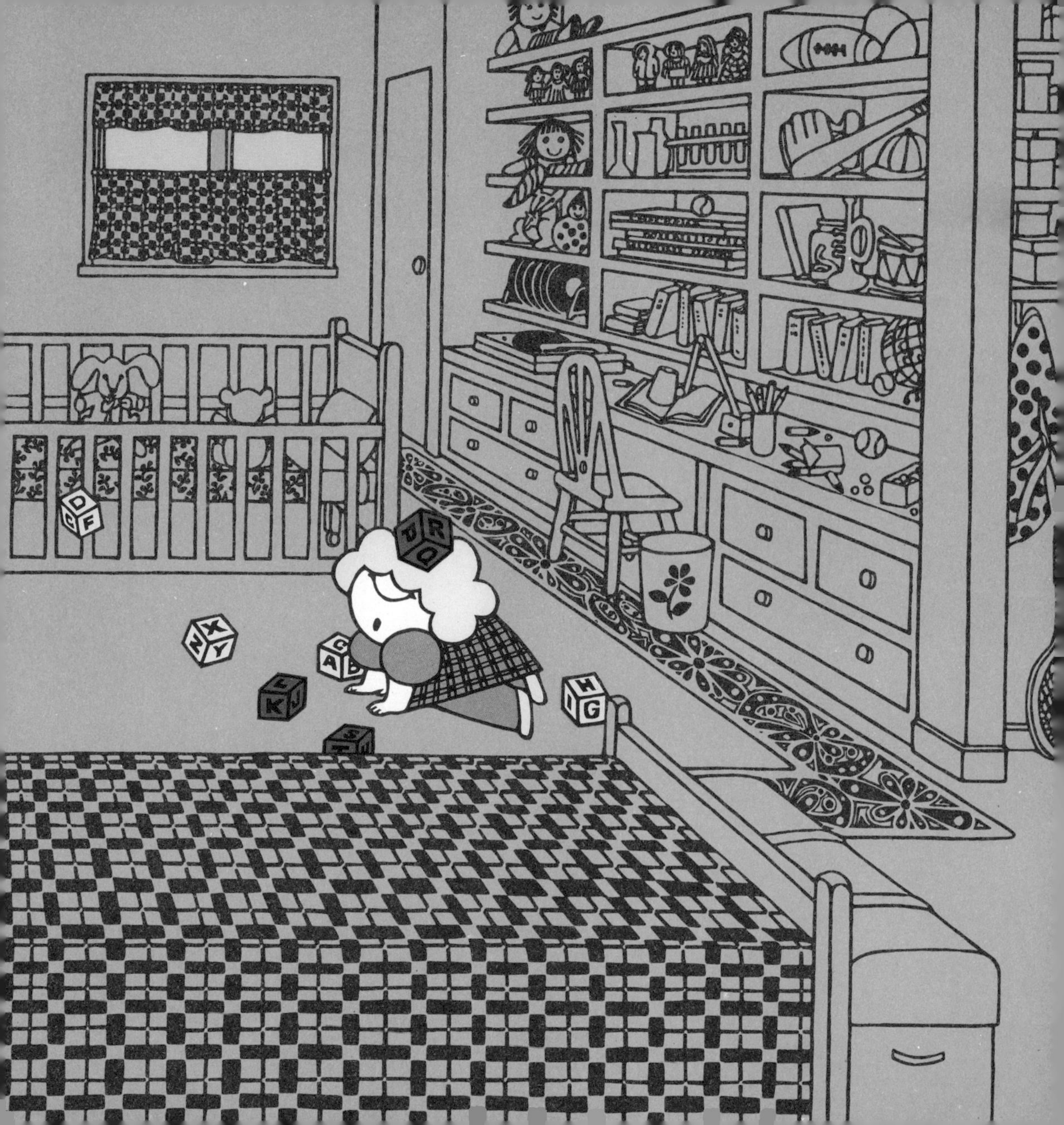

...knock, knock, rap, tap, ring, ring.

Sorry, Doris. I thought you could catch that block.

It didn't hurt much, and at least you know I am about.

When strange things begin to happen

everyone knows a poltergeist is about.

Except Harry who is too busy watching television.

Maybe he will notice me if I play the piano.

I'll just lift the piano top so he will hear me better.

Now what shall I play?

Tra, la, la, tra, la.

How about "The Flowers that Bloom in the Spring."

De dum dum, de dum dum, de dum, tra la...

Here is Harry, strong and able,
Father of Doris, dressed in plaid,
Father of Horace, good and bad,
Who lives in a four-room apartment.

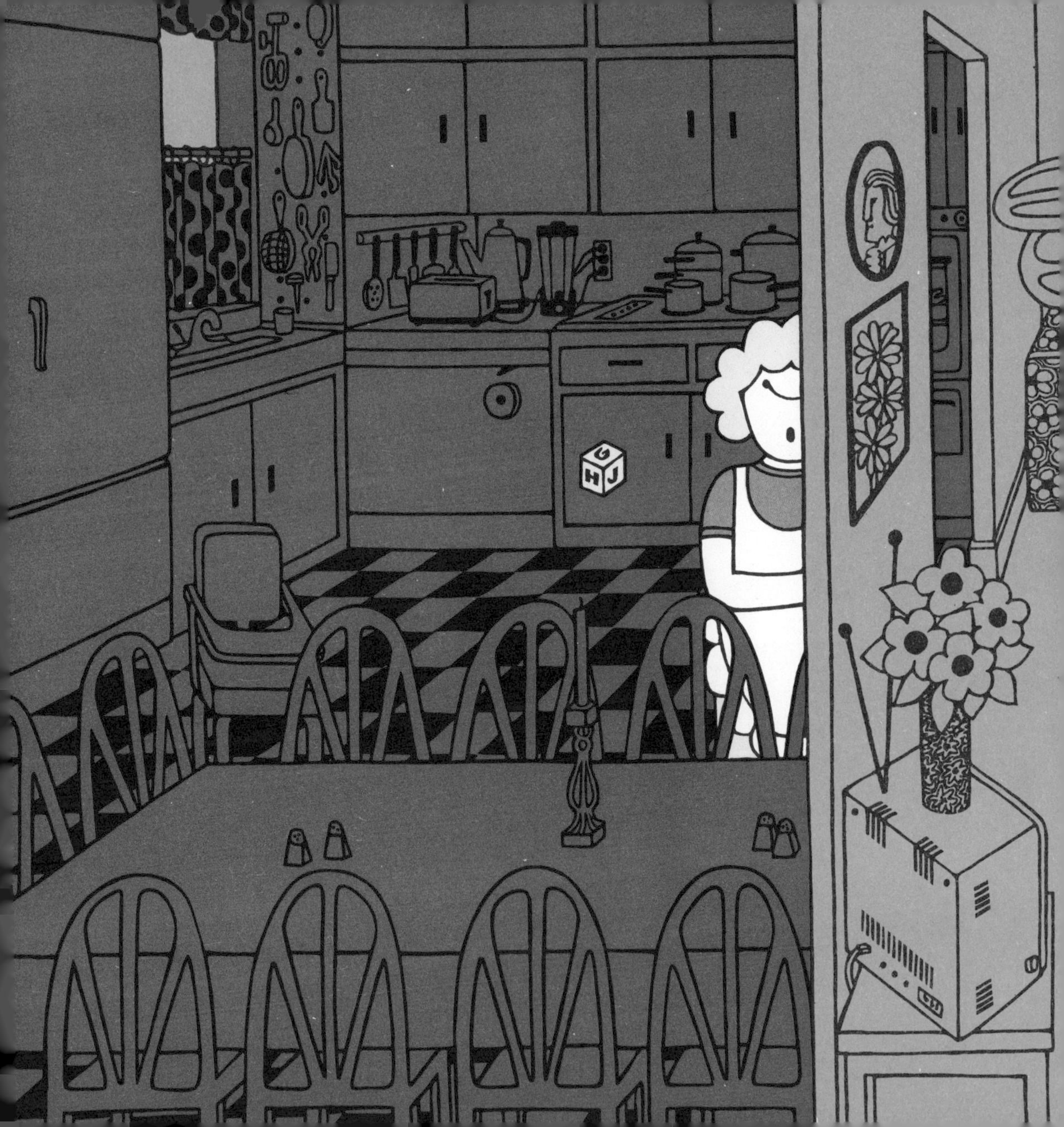
G
H
J

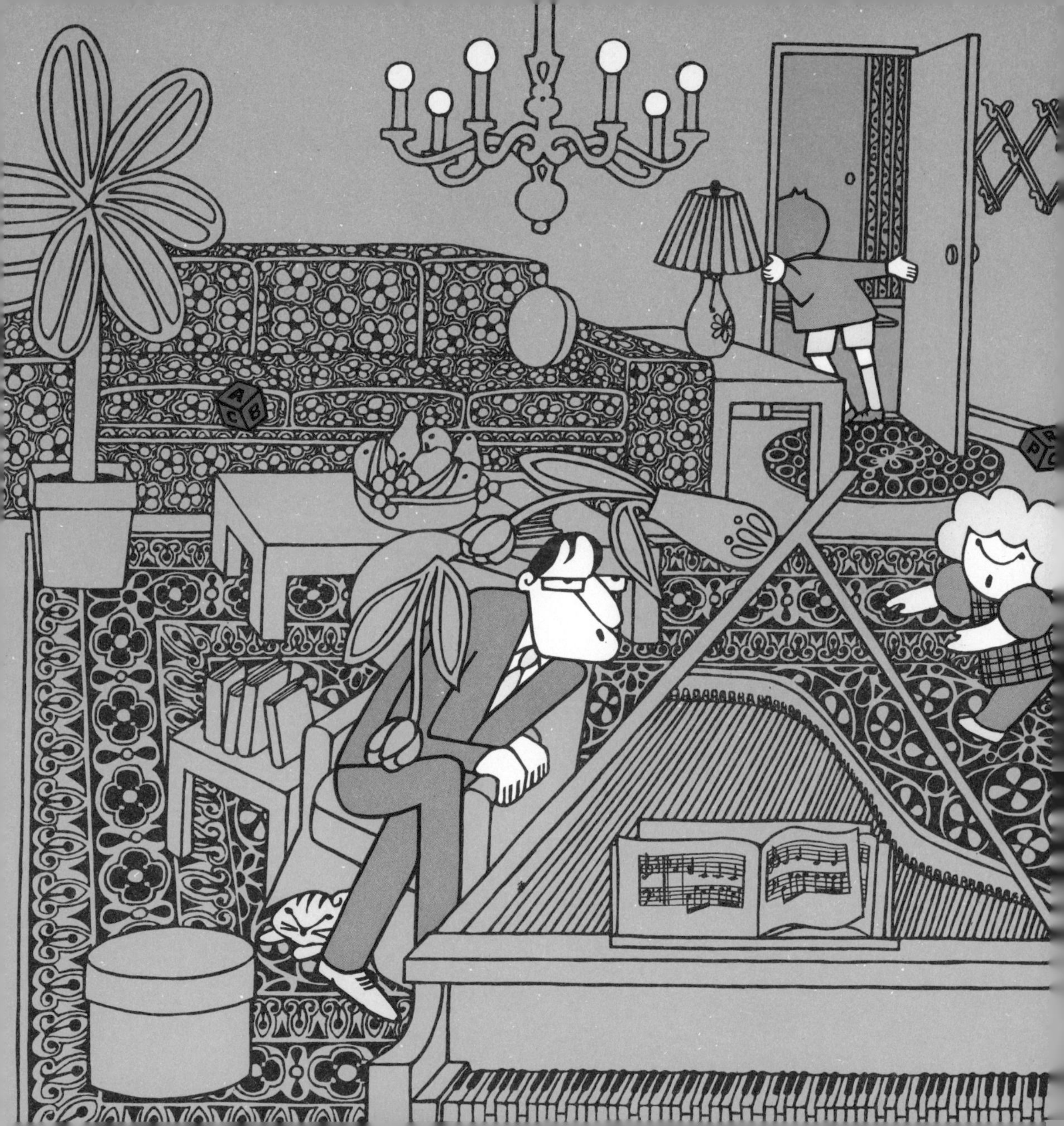

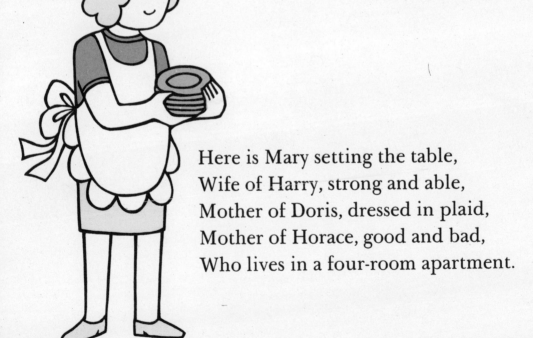

Here is Mary setting the table,
Wife of Harry, strong and able,
Mother of Doris, dressed in plaid,
Mother of Horace, good and bad,
Who lives in a four-room apartment.

...tra, la, la, tra, la, la, de dum.

Surprise, you never know where I'll turn up next.

All this rapping and tapping, knocking

and playing the piano has made me hungry.

I wonder if Mary has any mustard pickles.

I like watermelon rind and Tuscan peppers

but, most of all, I love mustard pickles.

In fact, I adore mustard pickles.

Rattle, bang, crash.

Only pots and pans in this cupboard, only cereal here.

Where are the mustard pickles?

Rattle, rattle, bang, crash...

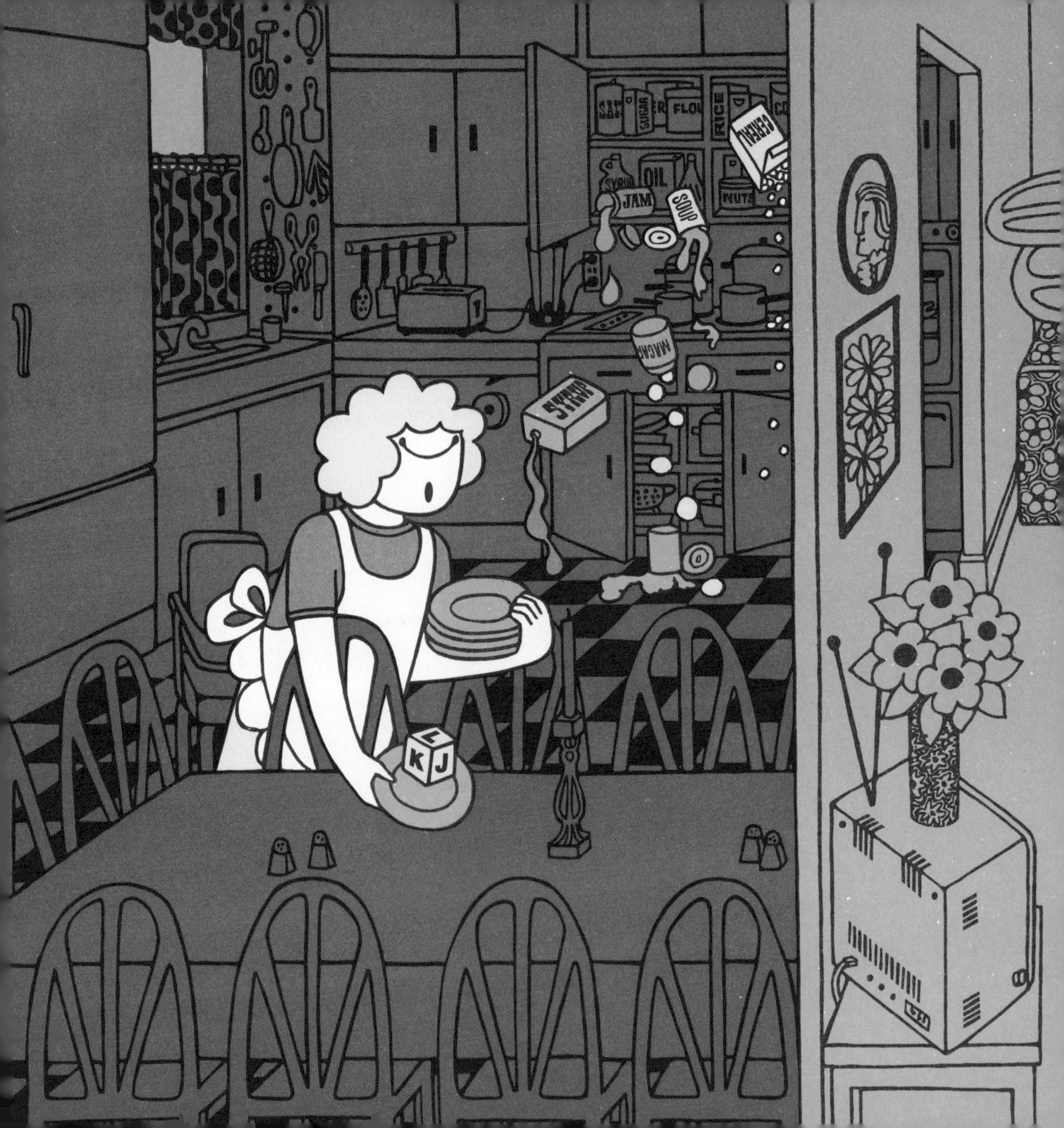
SUGAR
RICE
CEREAL
OIL
JAM
SOUP
NUTS
SYRUP
K
J
L

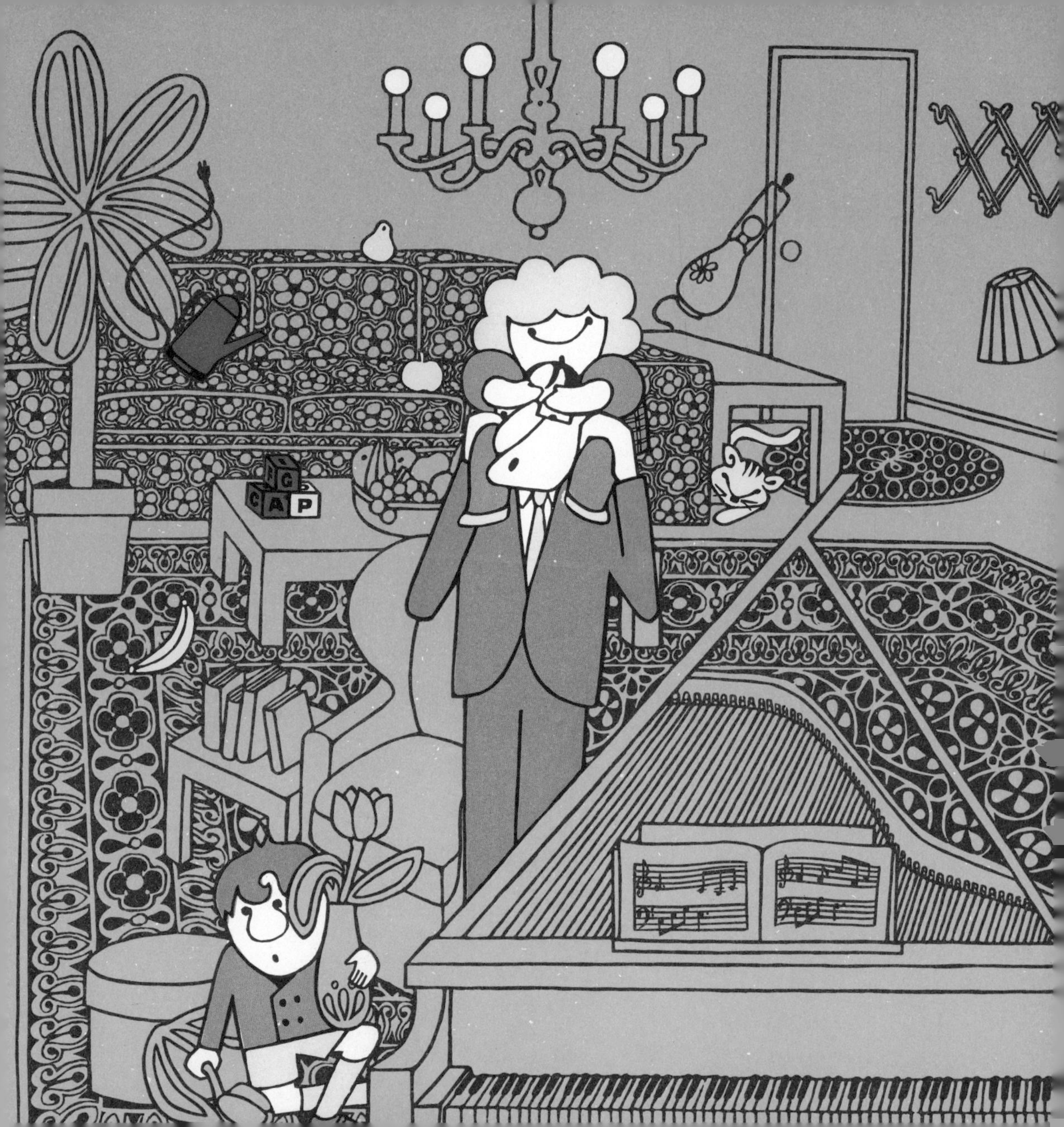
G
C A P

...crash, bang, rattle, rattle.

Now where can those mustard pickles be?

Poltergeists are quite expert

at opening cans and jars and popping bottle tops.

Pop! Pop! Pop!

Orange marmalade, olives stuffed with anchovies,

artichoke hearts and green turtle soup.

Everything here but mustard pickles.

If only I could read I wouldn't have to open every can.

Rap, tap, knock, knock.

Someone's at the door and it isn't me!

Bang, crash, pop, pop, pop...

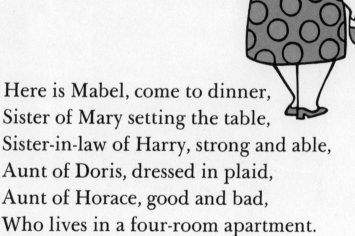

Here is Mabel, come to dinner,
Sister of Mary setting the table,
Sister-in-law of Harry, strong and able,
Aunt of Doris, dressed in plaid,
Aunt of Horace, good and bad,
Who lives in a four-room apartment.

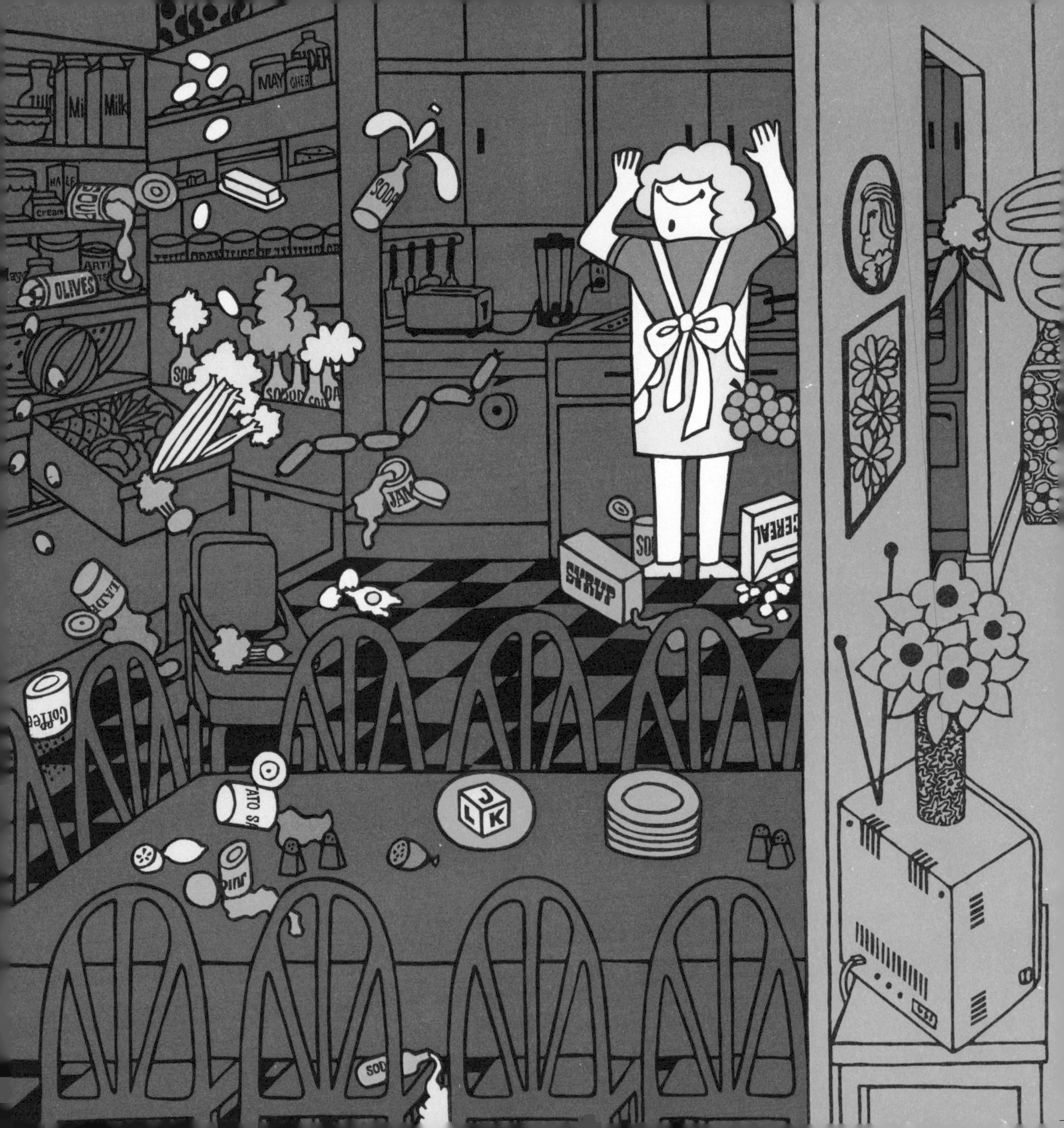
Milk
cream
MAY
OLIVES
SYRUP
JAM
Coffee

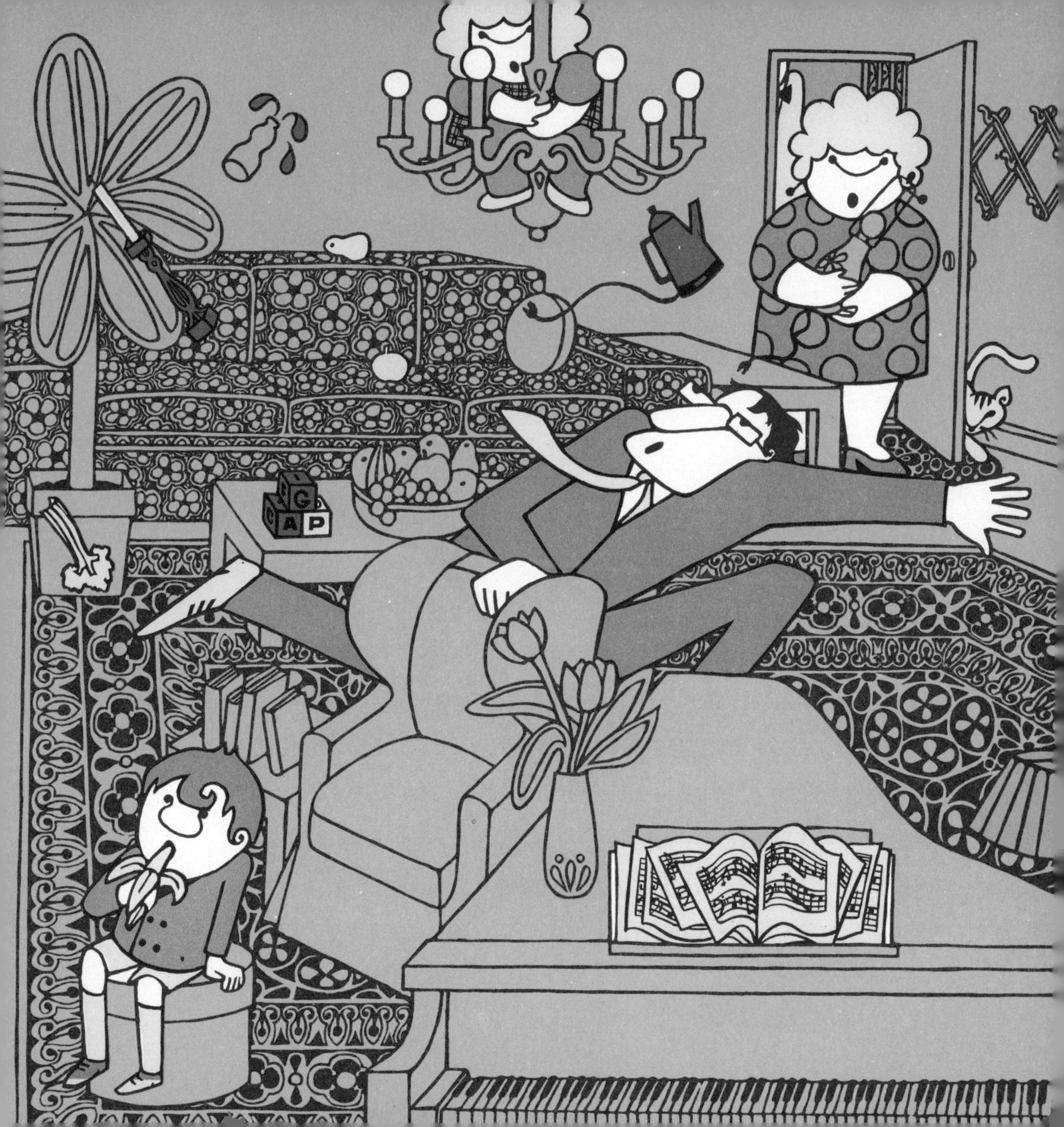
G
A P

Here is Abel, somewhat thinner,
Husband of Mabel, come to dinner,
Brother-in-law of Mary setting the table,
Brother-in-law of Harry, strong and able,
Uncle of Doris, dressed in plaid,
Uncle of Horace, good and bad,
Who lives in a four-room apartment.

...pop, pop, pop, bang, crash.

Abel is a nice man,

but I can't stand his wife Mabel.

She's always getting into my act.

First she goes rap, tap, knock, knock, on the door

and now she's playing piano.

And not very well, I must say.

Just for that I'll give them all a good scare.

Boo!

I wonder why everyone is afraid of the dark.

They can't see me in the light, either.

Boo, boo, whish, swish, boo...

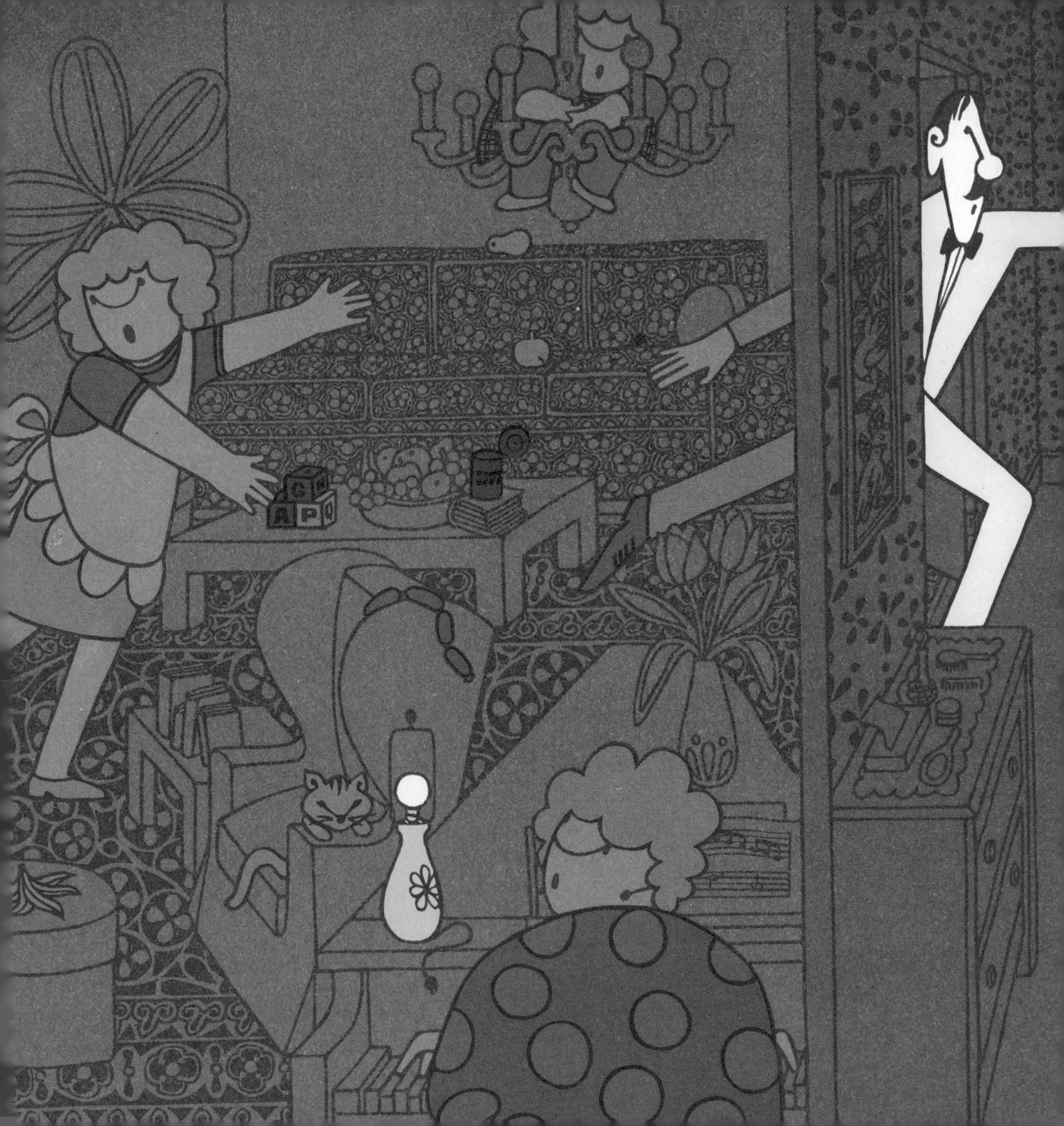

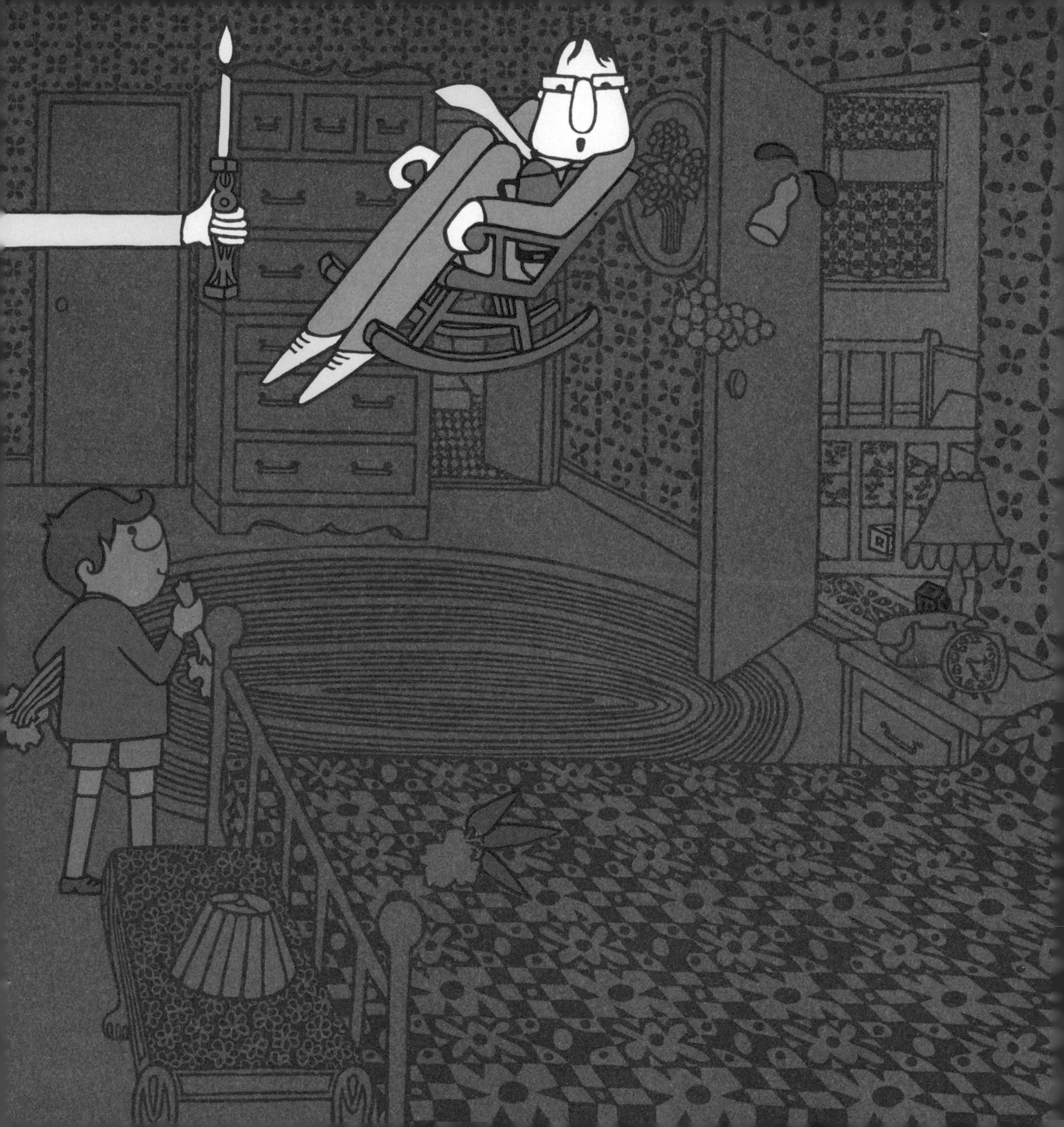

Here are the twins, Rachel and Ruth,
Daughters of Abel, somewhat thinner,
Daughters of Mabel, come to dinner,
Nieces of Mary setting the table,
Nieces of Harry, strong and able,
Cousins of Doris, dressed in plaid,
Cousins of Horace, good and bad,
Who lives in a four-room apartment.

...boo, whish, swish, boo, boo.

Horrors, I'm seeing double.

I had better turn on the lights again.

Horrors, I'm still seeing double.

Horrors, what noise these people make.

Poltergeists are supposed to be noisy,

but no one, except Horace, can hear my knocking

with all this racket going on.

How can I concentrate on finding my mustard pickles

with all this racket going on?

All right now, everybody, out of here! Quick!

Out, out, out, out, out...

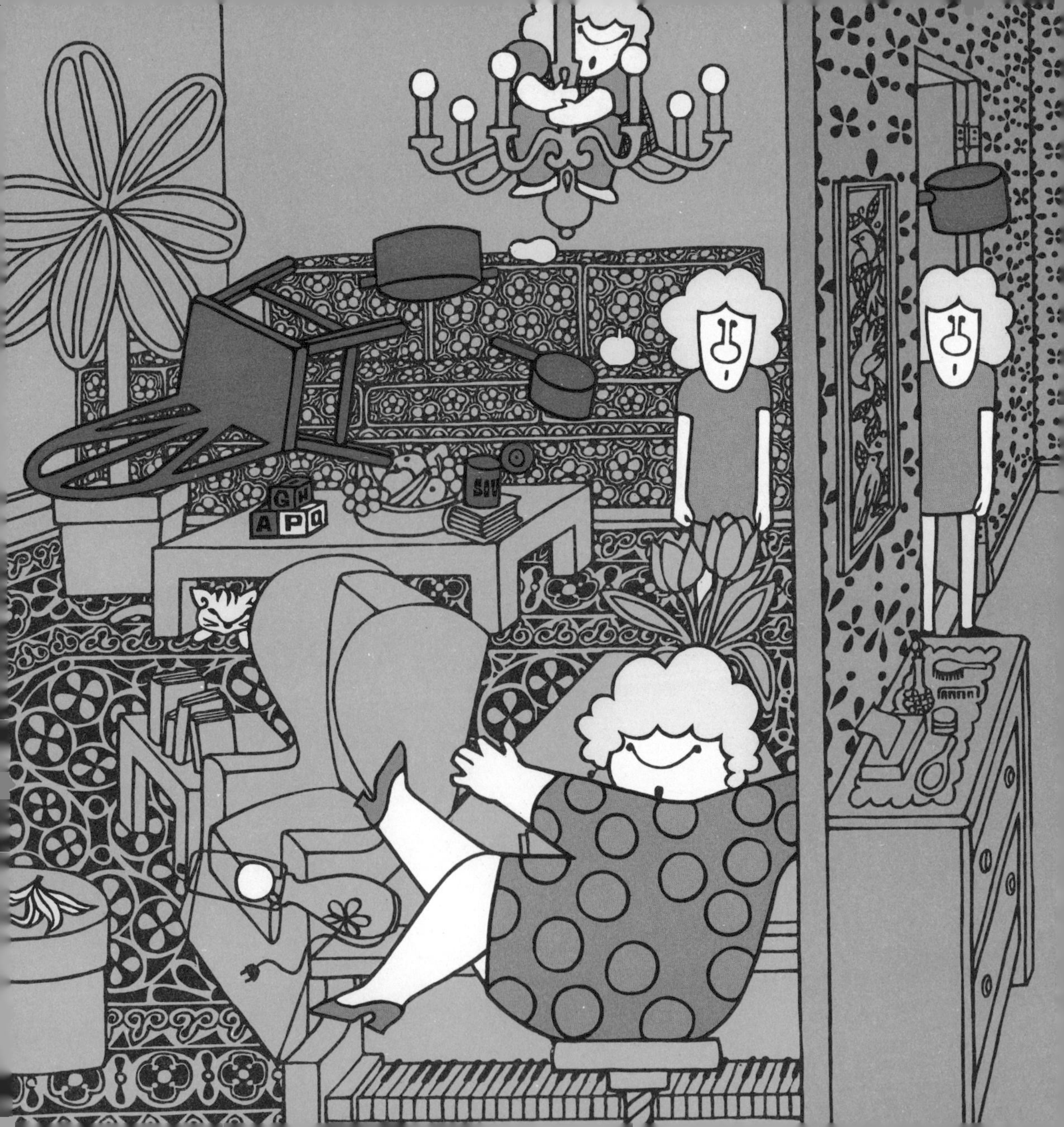
G H
A P Q

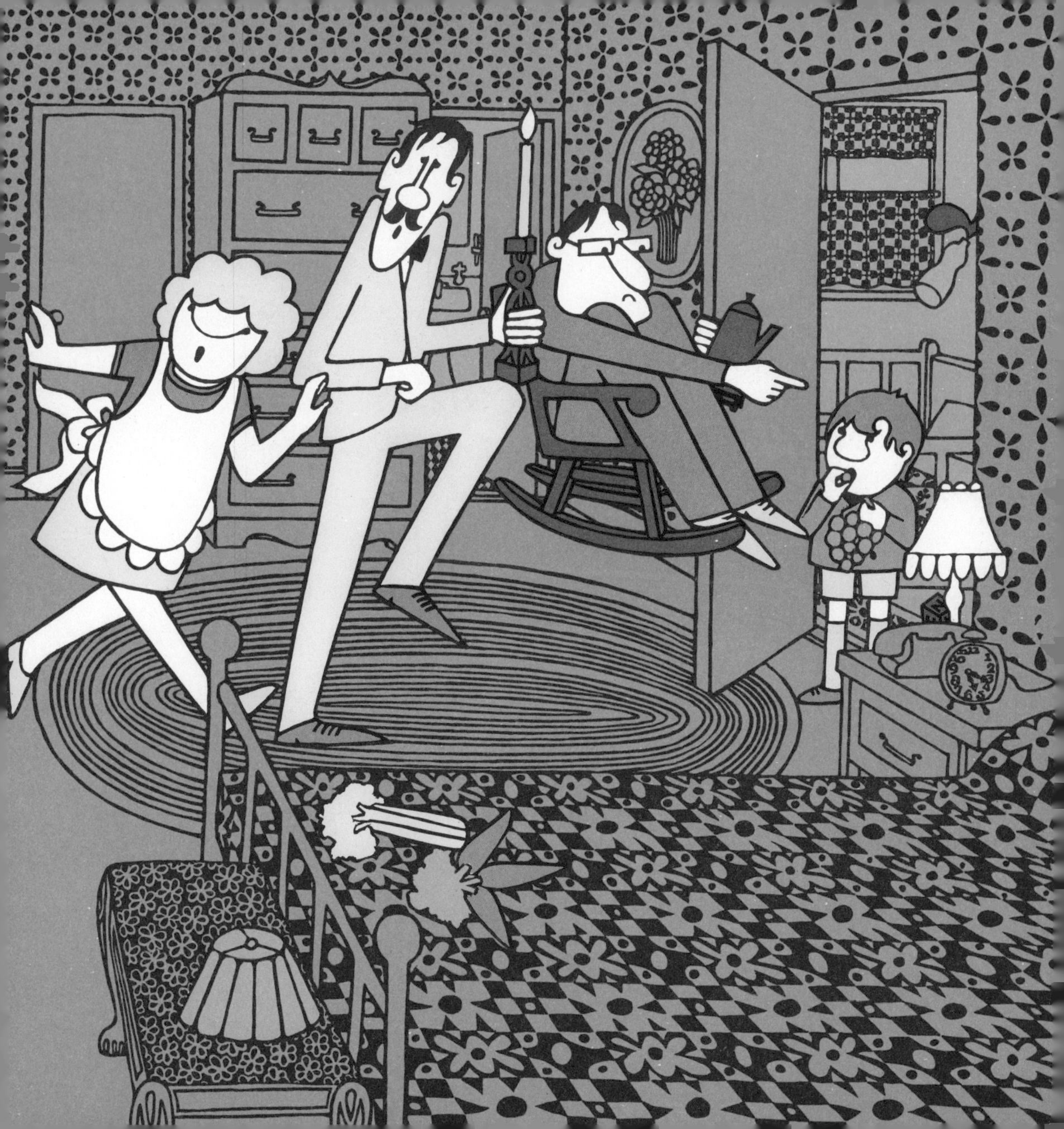

Here is Richard, missing a tooth,
Brother of twins, Rachel and Ruth,
Son of Abel, somewhat thinner,
Son of Mabel, come to dinner,
Nephew of Mary setting the table,
Nephew of Harry, strong and able,
Cousin of Doris, dressed in plaid,
Cousin of Horace, good and bad,
Who lives in a four-room apartment.

...*out, out, out, out, out!*

I did <u>not</u> knock out Richard's tooth.

Neither did Horace!

Hide, Horace, hide!

We try to have a little fun

and we get blamed for everything that goes wrong.

Just for that I'll show them

how a poltergeist can really play

when he sets his mind to it.

Hide, Horace, hide!

I'm going to show them how I play.

Hide, Horace, hide, hide, hide...

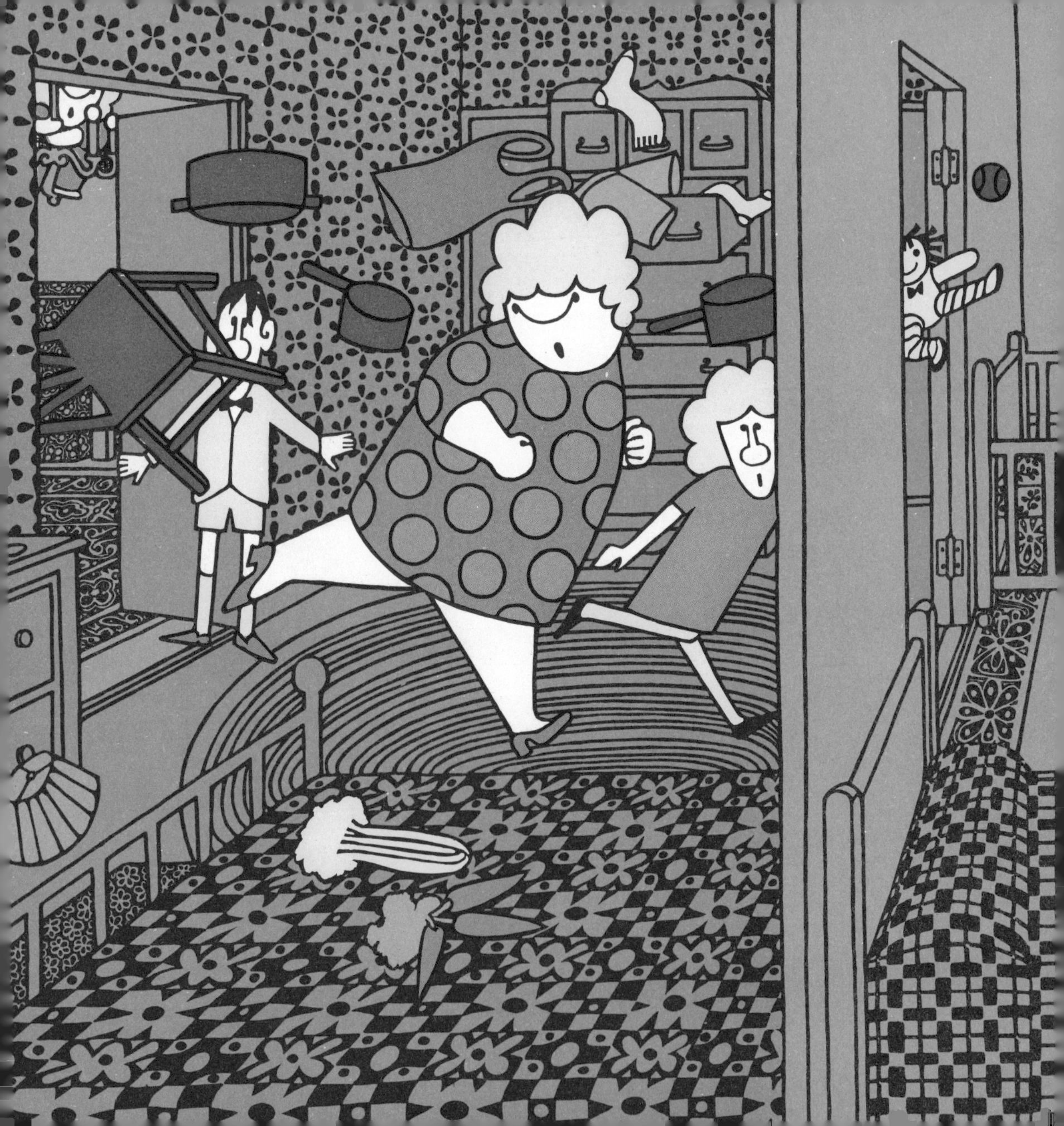

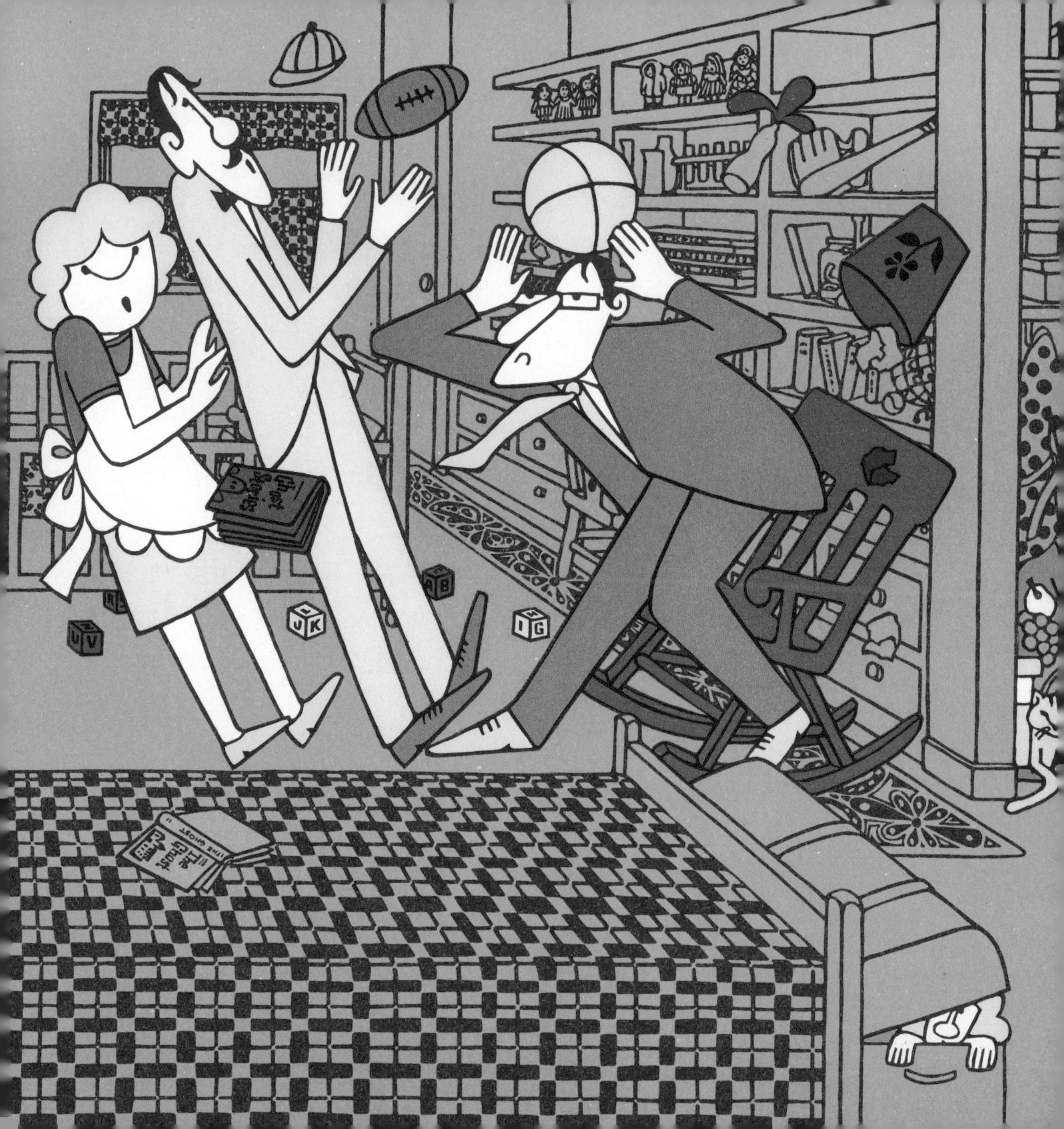
Ghost Stories
The Ghost

Here is Sarah, pleasingly plump,
Grandmother of Richard, missing a tooth,
Grandmother of twins, Rachel and Ruth,
Mother-in-law of Abel, somewhat thinner,
Mother of Mabel, come to dinner,
Mother of Mary setting the table,
Mother-in-law of Harry, strong and able,
Grandmother of Doris, dressed in plaid,
Grandmother of Horace, good and bad,
Who lives in a four-room apartment.

...hide, hide, hide.

Now why won't the family stay and play with me?

All they do is run back and forth,

back and forth, back and forth,

back and...Hello, who's here?

Why it's Grandmother Sarah.

I like Sarah. She is kind and wears hats.

I think everyone should wear hats.

Hats, hats, hats.

You don't have to hide anymore, Horace.

Come out and see everyone wearing a hat.

Hats, hats, hats, hats...

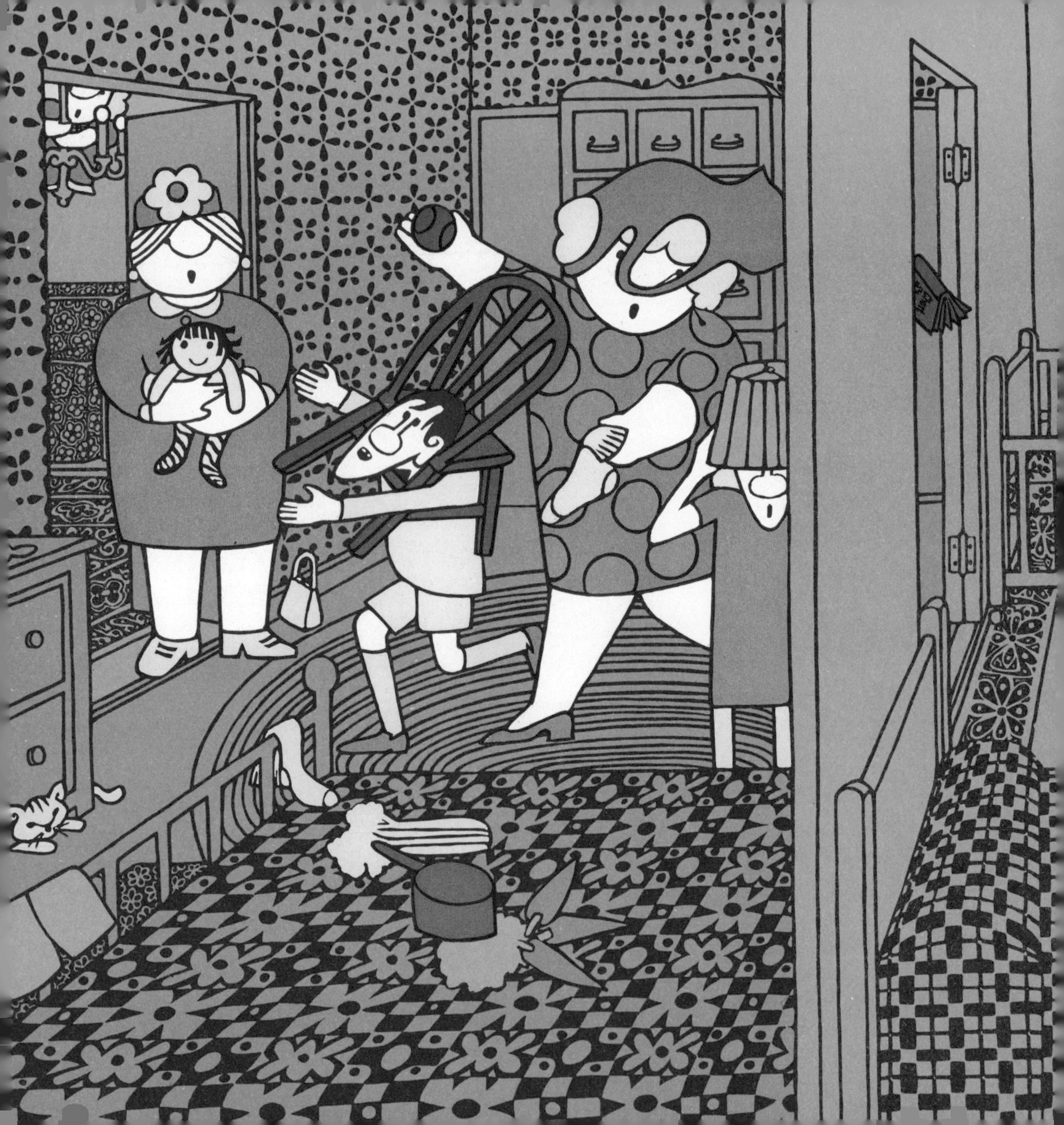

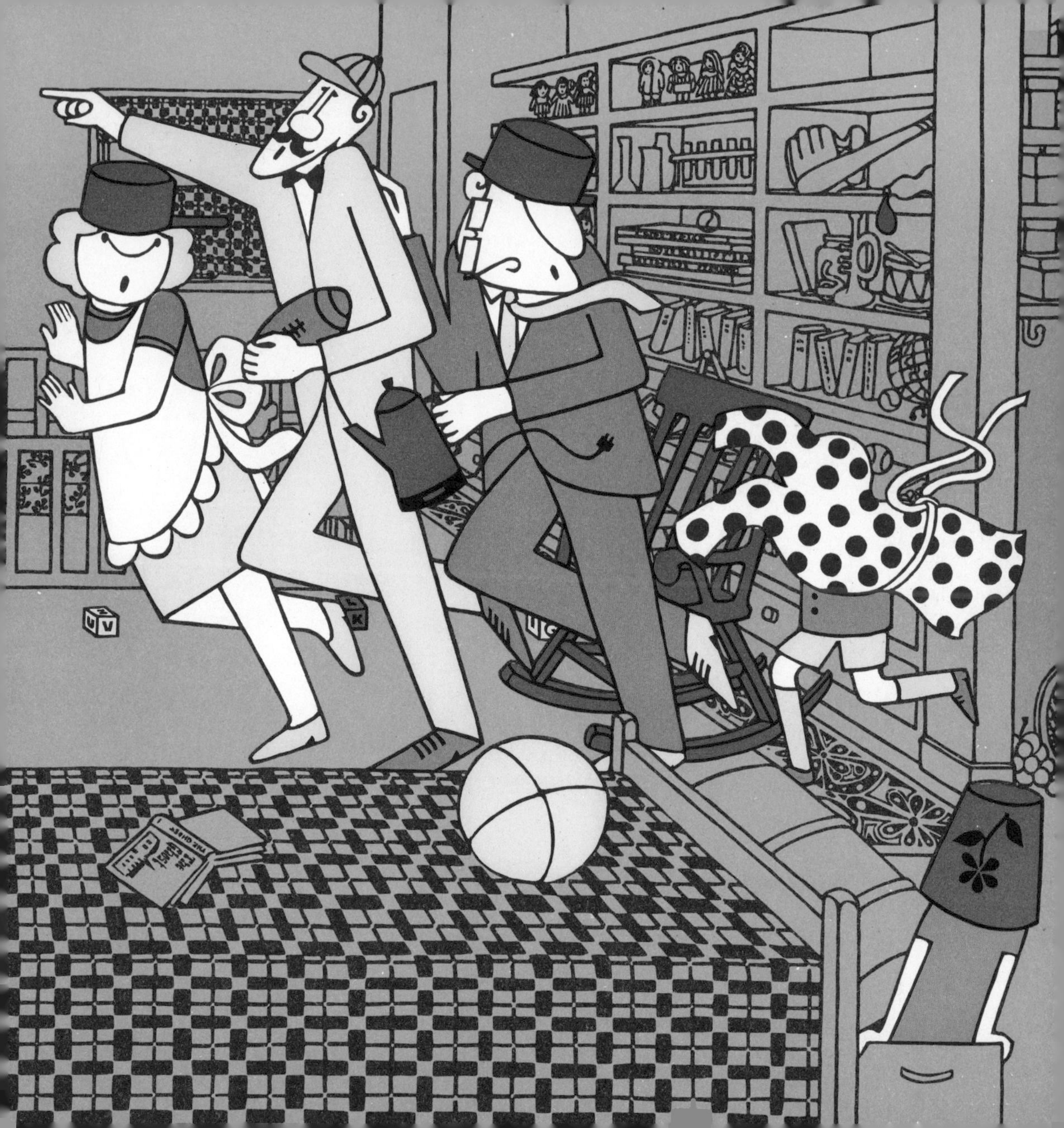

Here is Clara, getting a lump,
Unrelated to Sarah, pleasingly plump,
Unrelated to Richard, missing a tooth,
Unrelated to twins, Rachel and Ruth,
Unrelated to Abel, somewhat thinner,
Unrelated to Mabel, come to dinner,
Mother-in-law of Mary setting the table,
Mother of Harry, strong and able,
Grandmother of Doris, dressed in plaid,
Grandmother of Horace, good and bad,
Who lives in a four-room apartment.

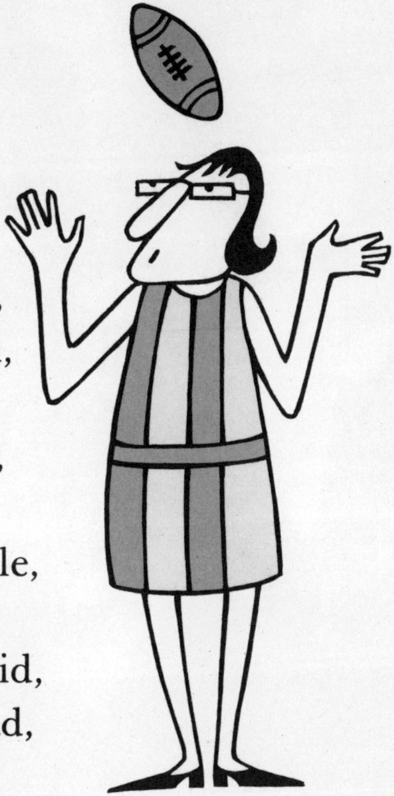

...hats, hats, hats, hats!

I must admit that maybe I am a bit mischievous.

But if I wasn't mischievous

then I wouldn't be a poltergeist.

And if I wasn't a poltergeist

then I wouldn't be a ghost.

And if I wasn't a ghost,

(and since no one can see me),

then who would I be? Not me!

Who, who, who?

Then whoever would I be?

Who, who, who, who...

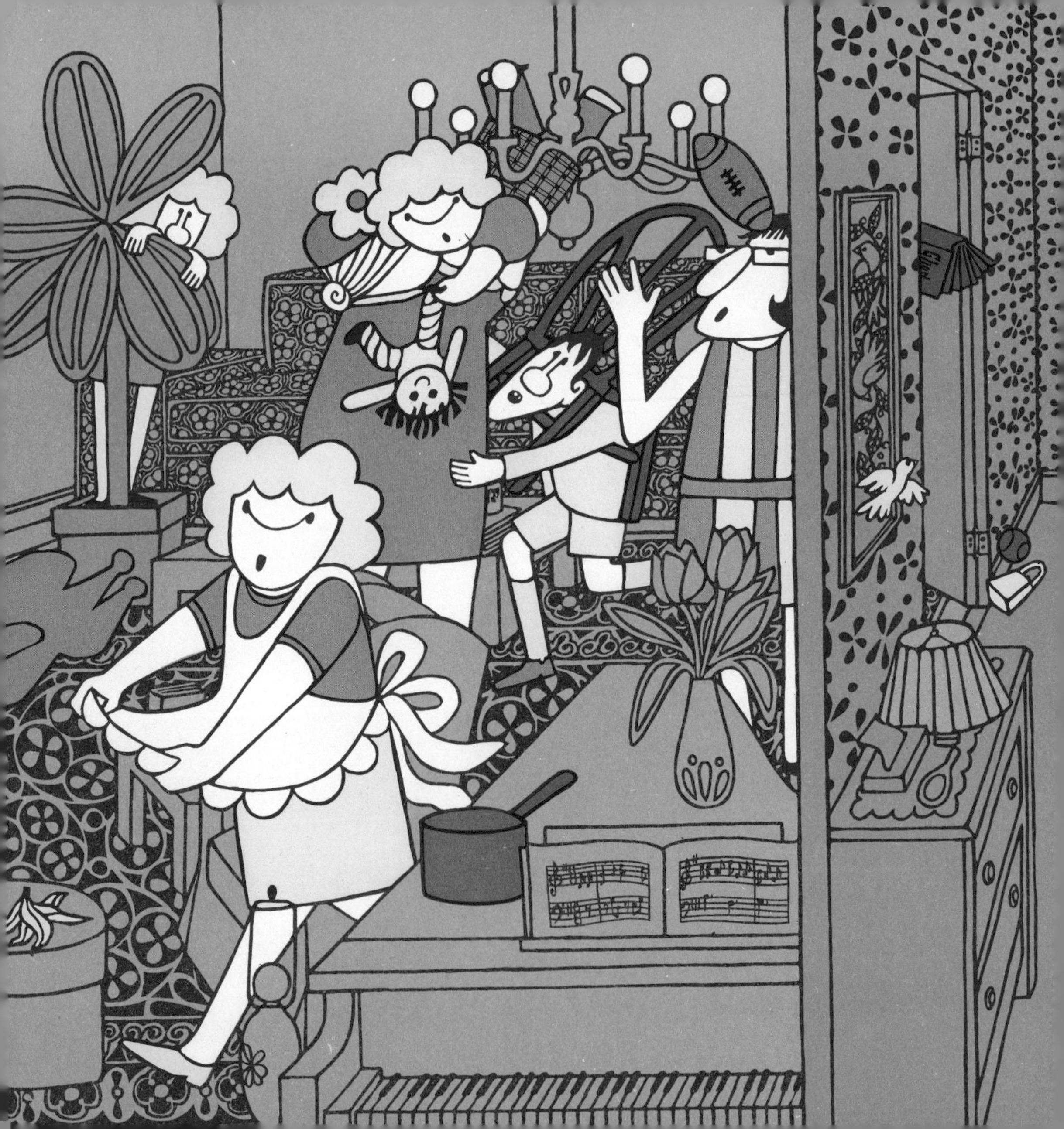

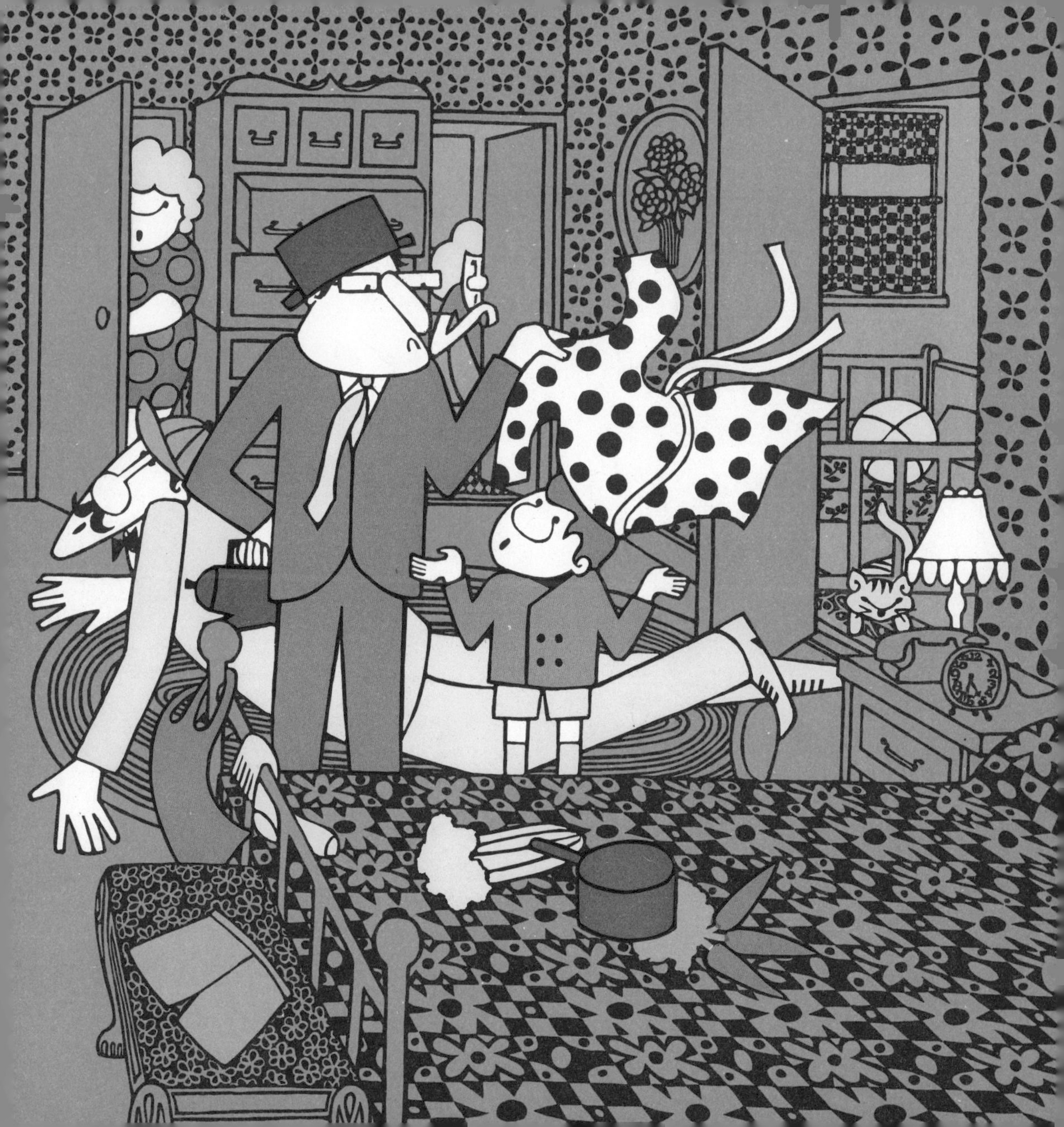

…who, who, who?

I may be a mischievous poltergeist,

but I don't enjoy getting my friends into trouble.

Poor Horace!

But look who's at the door.

Everything will be just fine now,

so I think I'll be on my way for Horace's sake.

Besides, this apartment is out of mustard pickles.

I wonder where I shall go now.

Where, where, where?

Do you have mustard pickles where you live?

Pickles, pickles, pickles, pickles…

Here is Boris,
Whose favorite is Horace.
Guess who he might be!

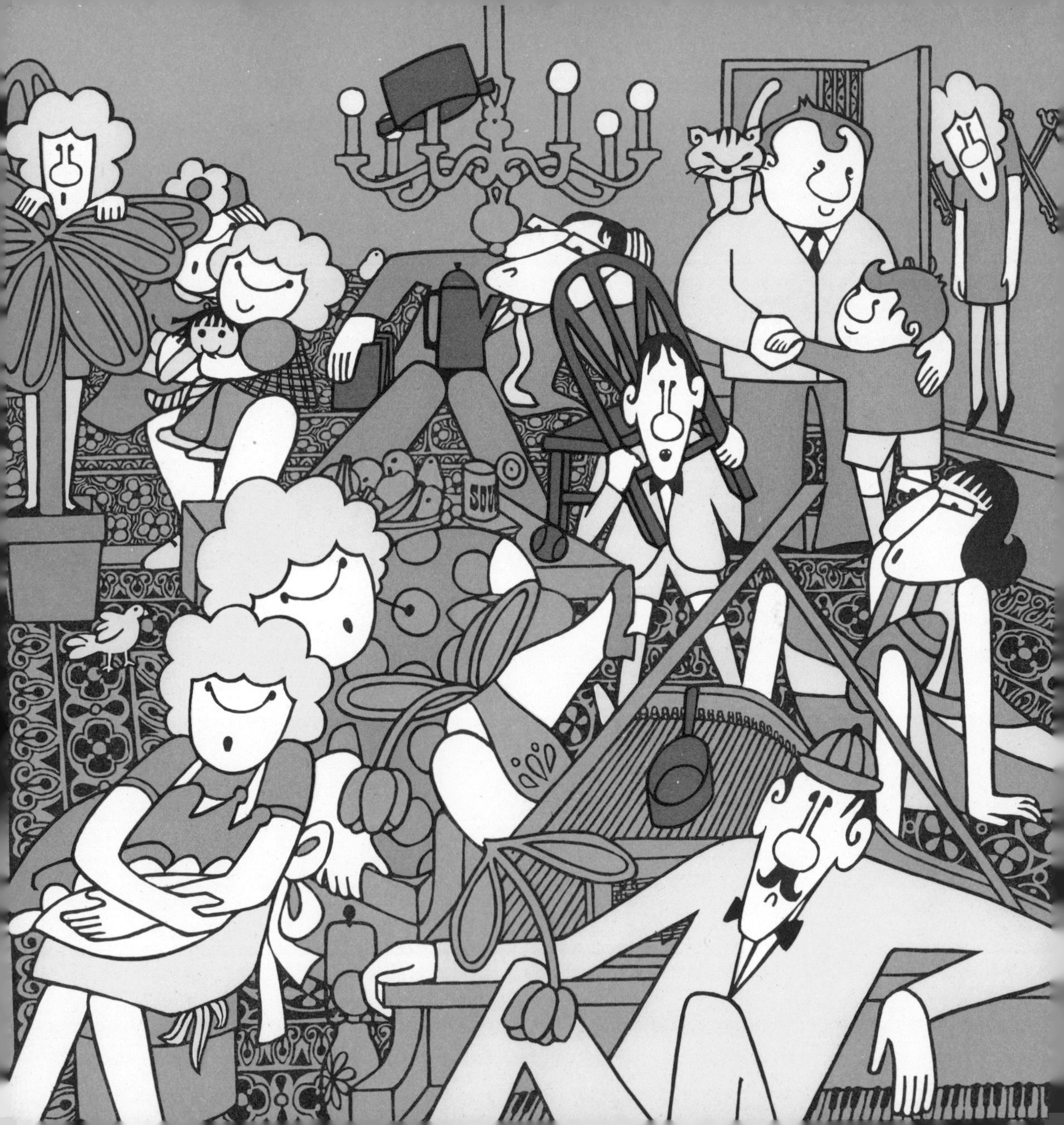